A LION AT BEDTIME

for Dad and Ben with love

Scholastic Children's Books,
Scholastic Publications Ltd,
7-9 Pratt Street, London NW1 0AE, UK

Scholastic Inc.,
730 Broadway, New York, NY 10003, USA

Scholastic Canada Ltd,
123 Newkirk Road, Richmond Hill,
Ontario, Canada L4C 3G5

Ashton Scholastic Pty Ltd,
PO Box 579, Gosford, New South Wales,
Australia

Ashton Scholastic Ltd,
Private Bag 1, Penrose, Auckland,
New Zealand

Published by Scholastic Children's Books

Copyright © by Debi Gliori 1993

ISBN: 0 590 54111 0

Typeset by Rapid Reprographics, London
Printed and bound in Hong Kong by Paramount Printing Group Limited

A LION AT BEDTIME

DEBI GLIORI

André Deutsch · Children's Books

Ben was a brave little boy.
"Fearless," said his father.
"Courageous," said his mother.
"Pushy," said the cows.

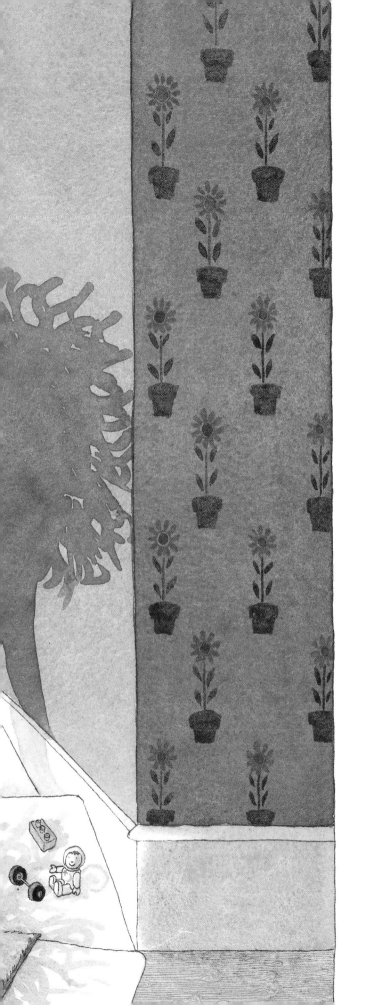

He was.
Except for the lion.
The lion that sneaked into
the house in the dead of
night, clackety-clawed its
way upstairs, paddy-pawed
along the corridor and into
Ben's bedroom.

Night after night the lion
came...

...and night after night Ben scrambled out of his own bed and into the safety of his parents' one.

"That smelly lion is here again," he would sob.

His mother told him that it was only a bad dream, and his father bumped about in the dark, banging doors and saying, "Right lion, back to the jungle. Scat, big cat!"

It usually took Ben and his parents a long time to get back to sleep.

One dark winter's night, with snow falling heavily and the wind roaring down the chimney pots,

Ben's lion opened the front door as usual, clackety-clawed up the stairs, paddy-pawed along the corridor

and came to a stop by Ben's bed. His paws were frozen stiff from walking in the snow and he really needed to get warm.

So he lifted a corner of the bedclothes and crawled in beside Ben.

Ben woke up. He was cold.

Something huge
and freezing and smelly
was in bed with him.

It was furry and breathing very loudly.

"The lion's in my bed!" he shrieked.
But Ben's father snored on. Tired out by too many lion-filled nights, he slept through Ben's cry.

The lion smiled toothily at Ben. He meant it to be a friendly smile,

but Ben thought it was the kind of smile a lion might give a boy before eating him. The lion opened his mouth wider.

"Yeeeuch," said Ben, "Your breath stinks!"
The lion looked at Ben with
huge yellow eyes. He was a
very handsome lion seen
close up.

He was shivering, though,
and Ben thought he might
be used to warm deserts and
steamy jungles, so was
probably feeling cold rather
than hungry.

"Lion, would you like me to warm you up?" he asked.

The lion nodded and gave a bed-shaking shiver.
"Follow me," said Ben,
"And I'll make you a hot drink
and find you something to wear."

Together they paddy-pawed   and clackety-clawed
downstairs. Ben gave the lion a drink of hot milk
and helped him to squeeze into a pair of his father's pyjamas.

"Now," said Ben firmly, "you're going to have to let me brush your teeth, if you're going to share my bed again."

The lion didn't know what tooth-brushing was, but he trusted Ben.
"All right," he said and carried Ben into the bathroom on his back.

Ben carefully brushed each of the lion's teeth in turn, until he could only smell the faintest hint of jungle through the mint of the toothpaste.

Back in bed, Ben and the lion curled up together. Soon all that could be heard over the howling wind was a small snoring and a deep growly purring.

Next morning Ben woke up, bounced onto his parents' bed, and told them all about the lion.
"I didn't hear you call out," said Dad.
"Neither did I," said Mum from deep under the bed clothes, "You were a brave boy not to wake us up, but to get rid of that smelly old lion all by yourself."

"He's not smelly any more," said Ben proudly.
"I brushed his teeth."

Dad went into the bathroom.

His toothbrush seemed to have lost most of its bristles
and Ben had used rather a lot of toothpaste
to remove the smell of the jungle.

At breakfast, Ben looked out of the kitchen window.
He saw a long trail of footprints
in the pillowy snow,

...and there was his lion smiling a dazzlingly white, minty smile.